A CLEVER CHRISTMAS BRIDE FOR THE BURDENED SHOP OWNER

THE TWELVE MAIL ORDER BRIDES OF CHRISTMAS

EMMA MORGAN

PURE READ

PUREREAD.COM

CONTENTS

.

ONCE UPON A CHRISTMAS ...

*C*allie bent over her suitcase, trying to figure out how she was going to get everything inside it. She had spent the previous evening sorting through her wardrobe, deciding what she would take and what she would leave behind. Even though she had pared down her gowns considerably, there still didn't seem to be enough room. Strands of her reddish brown hair had worked their way out of her braid and fell in her face. She blew them out of her way without stopping her task.

She had to get it done quickly, before the shock that she was running off as a mail order bride finished settling over her family. She'd given them the news over breakfast, as casual as if she had been speaking of buying a new pair of gloves. Aunt Abigail and Uncle Edward had been stunned into silence over their eggs and bacon. Callie hadn't given them much opportunity to argue. "It's all been settled," she'd said pleasantly but with authority. "I leave tomorrow." Her aunt and uncle had stared at her in surprise, but had made no arguments. She was old enough to make her own decisions now.

She heard soft footfalls on the stairs and her bedroom door creaked open behind her. "I suppose Aunt Abby told you," Callie said without turning around.

"I certainly wish I'd heard it from you, first," her sister Eliza replied. "We could have talked about it before you made any rash decisions."

Callie straightened up and turned to face her sister. She narrowed her green eyes at her, irritated that they would be having one of these conversations again. "I don't need your approval, Eliza. I might be younger than you, but I am fully capable of making my own decisions."

"But a mail order bride?" Eliza nearly wailed. "Why on earth would you do such a thing? It isn't as though you can't find a husband here in Philadelphia."

Callie shook her head and returned to packing. "This really isn't about a husband, Eliza. I'm going to cancel the contract as soon as I arrive."

"What?" Her sister sat on the bed so she could still look into Callie's face. "Surely that's not a moral thing to do."

Callie sighed. "It happens all the time, Eliza. The man doesn't need to know that I never intended to fulfill my end of the bargain. I'll come up with an excuse and it'll be over with. Like I said to Aunt and Uncle, it's all been settled. I'm going to Wyoming."

Eliza was not done arguing, however. "If you aren't even going to marry this man, then what's ... oh. I understand. This is about that silly writing thing, isn't it? Callie, you have a perfectly good job in our general store. You can write in the evenings."

Callie scowled at the spare boots she was shoving into the corner of the suitcase. "Don't call it a silly writing thing. You know it has always been my dream to write a book. And no, I can't do it here. Between helping you and Ned run the store, and then my responsibilities here at home, there simply isn't the time or the energy to write."

"But you *do* write, all the time," Eliza protested.

"What, those silly signs for the store window? I can promise you it doesn't take any great talent to come up with a simple advertising scheme for a general store."

At first, Callie had jumped at the opportunity to work at the store that her sister and her new husband owned. It would give her time away from home, and she had hoped she might feel inspired by the goings-on of the numerous customers that came in every day. But she soon discovered that she was too busy to come up with anything even worthy of being written down. She had created a few signs promoting sale items or new inventory, but it was out of sheer boredom more than anything.

"Well, I don't know who's going to make them once you're gone. Ned has his hands full keeping up with the inventory and the cash register, and once the baby arrives I won't be any use to him at all." Eliza ran her hands over her swollen stomach.

Callie nodded. "Which means I'll have even less time to write. I don't envy you one of those, sister. There is certainly no room in my life for children. And you can just reuse the signs I've already made." She closed the suitcase and buckled it.

"You can't just run away from your responsibilities, Callie. What are you going to do when you're in the middle of nowhere and you've cancelled the marriage contract with your intended? You'll be a woman alone in the wilderness. Think of all the things that could happen to you!" Eliza put a hand to her cheek in horror.

"Nothing will happen to me." Callie pulled the suitcase off her bed and set it on the floor with a thump. "I'll move to the next town over so I don't have to see the poor man on a regular basis. I'll take some time for myself and finally do what I want to do. The next time you see me, I'll have written a book."

"We'll see," Eliza said as she swept out of the room. She turned around in the hallway with a final thought. "You'll be missing Christmas!"

Callie shut her bedroom door.

The train slowed to a crawl as it pulled into the station in Cheyenne. Callie was grateful that the long trip was finally over. She had been fortunate enough to have a sleeper car, but she still felt as though she hadn't been able to truly move around for over two days. Her knees ached from sitting and her neck hurt from staring out the window most of the time. The pain helped fuel the strength she would need when she emerged onto the platform. Her intended would be there waiting for her, and she wouldn't like him. He would probably be a rough and dirty rancher, smelling of cattle and barely civilized. It would be easy to break off their deal at first sight. Then she could flag down a coach to carry her and her bags to the next town to start her new life.

The swarm of people on the platform was overwhelming. The steam of the engine and the dust from the tracks added to the confusion as she wandered aimlessly, searching for someone who seemed to be searching for her. She noted a few cowboys, but they were occupied with unloading shipments that had come in on the train or had already found their brides.

After a few minutes, Callie tired of searching. She spotted a kind-looking gentleman standing patiently at the edge of the platform. His sandy blonde hair matched his mustache, which half hid a pleasant smile as he surveyed his surroundings patiently.

"Excuse me, sir. I'm looking for Will Stanton. Do you know him?" she asked.

"I certainly do. I know him quite well, actually. I'm Will Stanton." He paused to smile at the look of surprise on Callie's face, his blue eyes glittering. "And I imagine you must be Miss Callie Browning. It is my absolute pleasure to meet you." He swept off his hat and bowed to her.

Completely taken aback, Callie wasn't sure what to do. This man wasn't the uncivilized monster she'd imagined, not by a long shot. She thought she would have a reason to run off to the next town immediately, but there was certainly none here. His clothes were clean and neatly patched, and he didn't smell like cattle at all. He even had the nerve to be handsome. She managed to mutter, "How do you do?" before Will graciously scooped up her suitcase and offered his elbow to escort her to his wagon.

"Welcome to Cheyenne, Miss Browning," he said as they stepped out onto the main street where his wagon sat. "Although I suppose I'm not much of a welcoming committee, having only been here a few years myself." He gently placed her suitcase in the back before helping her climb up onto the seat.

"And what brought you to this area?" Callie asked, feeling rather uncertain of herself.

"The train, like most folks," he laughed. His cheeks flushed and Callie had to blink to stop herself from staring at him. "Seriously, though," he continued, "when the transcontinental railroad came through, it seemed like the perfect place to set up shop. Lots of folks come through here every day, and it's a nice town. I wanted to be out West, but I wasn't too interested in mining for gold or running a ranch. No, my heart has always been yearning for a general store."

"Oh." Callie's heart fell through the wooden board underneath her. She could have turned to him right then and there and told him to take her back to the train station immediately. He seemed like a kind enough man that he would probably do it, but there was just something about him that made her wait.

I need a really good reason to leave, she thought. Otherwise he'll know I never meant to stay.

"We'll go on home so you can get settled in. I figured you'd want to have an actual wedding ceremony instead of getting married at the courthouse, you being from Philly and all, so we'll need to wait until after Christmas. This is our busy season, after all."

Callie nodded, staring at the ground in thought. *At least that gives me some time.*

"Oh, but don't worry," Will continued. "My aunt lives in our house, too, so you don't have to worry about anything being improper."

"Oh, yes. Yes, of course," she muttered.

By this time they had reached Stanton's General Store. Callie eyed the tall wooden façade with large windows. It could have been a dead ringer for Ned's store, save for the mountainous backdrop in the distance. She eyed it with disgust, but kept her tongue.

"Well, here we are. Home, sweet home. The house is attached to the back of the store. It's mighty convenient." He pulled her suitcase out of the wagon with ease and pushed through the front door. "I'm home!" he called to the empty store as Callie came in behind him.

The shelves that lined the walls were straight and even, all their contents facing the same direction and neatly stacked. Stacks of crates and barrels filled in any space that wasn't already taken up by shelving. The floor was worn in spots but immaculate. Callie surveyed the perfect little store with dread. Will would probably have her working the counter first thing tomorrow, and she would be right back where she had been.

Alright, now I have a reason to leave. Not one that will seem particularly good to anyone else, but good enough to me.

Just then a door at the back of the store burst open. A young boy, about six years old, came strolling through, a wobbling toddler holding his hand. The boy had the same sandy blonde hair and blue eyes as his father. The toddler's face was half-hidden by her bonnet, which had gone askew. Perfect blonde ringlets sprung out around the eyelet edges. She and her older brother surveyed Callie with curiosity.

Will introduced them. "This is my son, Alexander, and my daughter, Rachel."

He stood back to watch the scene unfold between his children and his wife-to-be, but Callie remained rooted to the wooden floor. The children mumbled polite hellos, the little girl's nothing more than babble, but Callie made no move to embrace them or shake their hands or whatever else Will might have expected.

"Children, why don't you go see if Aunt Mary's awakened up from her nap yet. It'll be supper time soon." The children scuttled back through the door, and Will turned to Callie, a nervous grin on his face. "I know. I didn't say anything about the children in my advertisement. I do apologize. A friend of mine told me that women prefer to have their own children, instead of raising someone else's. I thought … I thought you might not come if you knew we were already a family."

Callie only stared at him.

"My wife died, you see. She became very ill last year. There are some good doctors here, and I brought them all to see her. They did what they could, but she didn't make it. It's been very hard to take care of the children and run the store, even with Aunt Mary here. She's a dear, but she can't do much." He looked up at Callie with watering eyes. "My children need a mother, Callie."

She blinked back tears of her own and nodded. She felt her throat tighten at the realization of all that she would need to do if she were to stay with this man. The store would be bustling all day with customers, the bell over the door ringing every time someone walked in or out. Someone would have to work the counter and keep up with the inventory. Callie would have to get up early to make breakfast, and as soon as she finished cleaning up it would be time to make the next meal. Life in this place would be solid work and noise. There would be no writing for her here, not at all.

I can't go anywhere tonight. I'll find a way to leave in the morning. Finally, she nodded at Will and stepped through the door into her new home.

The morning dawned cold and bright. Callie dragged herself out from under the pile of quilts on her bed reluctantly. She had the children up and breakfast started before she realized that Will was nowhere to be seen.

"Where's your father gone off to?" she asked Alexander, who sat patiently waiting at the table for his food. Rachel sat in the chair next to him, happily playing with a spoon.

"Fiddling with his silly store," Aunt Mary answered before the child had a chance. She sat in her rocking chair by the fire, the only place that Callie had seen her since she'd arrived. Her old, withered face was partially obscured by her bonnet, but Callie could see the contempt on it. "He's always in there playing, instead of doing real work."

Will had told Callie that Aunt Mary liked to ramble and not to worry about what she might say, but Callie was curious. "And what would real work be?"

Aunt Mary shook her grey head. "Lots of things. Farming, building something, surviving. Not catering to other folks. When I was young, I ..." Mary trailed off as she fell asleep, which seemed to be a normal state for her.

Callie shook her head in amusement and turned back to the boy at the table. "So when do you plan on decorating your tree over there?" Her hands busy stirring a pot of porridge, she nodded at the evergreen that stood in the corner. "It's getting awful close to Christmas."

Alexander looked at her solemnly. "We don't have any decorations for it, ma'am."

Callie continued to stir the porridge furiously. None of what happened here in this house should have mattered to her—she would be leaving soon anyway—but the idea of a bare Christmas tree pricked underneath her skin like pine needles. Maybe Will should be tending to his children's Christmas some more, and thinking of them instead of spending all his time in the store. She poured a bowl of porridge for each of the children and for Aunt Mary before stalking into the store.

Will was behind the counter, examining a ledger book. He jumped at the thump of the door behind him as Callie entered. The shop wasn't officially open yet; the front door was still locked.

"I'd like to talk to you, Will," she demanded.

"Oh, good morning. Yes. Yes, of course," he replied, closing the ledger book and putting it on a shelf below the counter.

"Why on Earth don't you have any Christmas decorations on that tree?" When she only got a look of further surprise from him, she continued. "You own a general store. You can order crates of whatever you like, and yet those babies have a bare tree?"

Callie burned inside and tried to stand firm. This conversation was supposed to be about her leaving. This was when she was supposed to find a good reason to leave, and the silly tree didn't seem to be enough. Looking around his store more closely, she realized the problem didn't stop at the tree.

"You don't even have your store decorated? I know you're out in the West here, Will, but surely you know how all the stores back east do it. There's not a single item in your front windows to even suggest its Christmas."

"Oh." Will looked at the store around him and scratched the back of his head. "Well, ah, I have ordered some decorations, you see, but the shipments are running behind. Big demand of the holidays and all. Not much I can do about that. It takes forever to get anything out West." He laughed, but it was a forced laugh. Will quickly turned his back to her and straightened a display of spice jars that already seemed quite neat.

Callie pursed her lips in thought. There was something odd here, but she couldn't quite put her finger on it.

It's not really my business anyway, since I'm leaving.

"Very well," she heard herself say, "I'll take care of it." She marched back through the door, trying to hide her surprise at herself.

Fortunately, she had closed the door before Will had a chance to question her on her plans, but she doubted he was going to. He was a nice man, but he wasn't very bold.

She shrugged. She said she was going to take care of it, so take care of it she would. She headed into the kitchen and began rummaging through the cupboards until she had everything she needed.

"Children?" she called.

It didn't take long for Alexander to come running, Rachel in tow. "Yes, ma'am?"

"How would you like to make some Christmas decorations with me?" Callie smiled at them, feeling an unexpected excitement build up inside her.

Alexander, however, seemed more uncertain. "I don't know how, ma'am."

Her heart reached out to this miniature version of his father. "Don't worry about that; I'll help you. Here, you two sit at the table and you can help me put all the ingredients in the mixing bowl."

Before long, they had made a large batch of gingerbread dough. Alexander carefully cut stars and bells out of the rolled-out dough with a cookie cutter, the tip of his tongue sticking out in concentration. Rachel happily played in the flour, dipping her hands in it and then clapping them together, laughing at the swirl of powder she created in the air. Callie made a small hole in the top of each cookie so they would be able to tie them to the tree later.

Next they moved on to stringing popcorn and cranberries. Callie had to do most of the work herself, not feeling that either of the children were quite ready to handle a sharp needle. But the boy handed Callie kernels and berries one at a time and helped make sure the newly-made garland didn't get tangled. The baby mouthed a cranberry and promptly spit it back out, but she oohed and aahed at the end result as Callie draped it across the boughs of the tree.

Hours later, Callie stood back to survey her work, her arms across the shoulders of each of the children. These decorations had taken a lot of time, but it hadn't felt like work. It had been fun and relaxing, despite the mess they had made. She remembered doing just this sort of thing with her sister when they were little, and a warm, happy feeling settled in her stomach. She tried to shake it off, reminding herself that she didn't belong here. But for at least a little bit, it felt as though she did.

She heard the door open behind her as Will came in from the shop.

Is it that late already?

Her back tensed, waiting for a reprimand for wasting the day with crafts when they could have been cooking, cleaning, or helping out with the shop. She didn't turn around, but kept a hand on each of the children and waited.

Will's footsteps creaked across the wooden floor, stopping just beside her.

"That looks mighty fine," he said. "Mighty fine."

Later that evening, Callie settled down in a chair by the fire. Supper had been served and cleaned up. She had changed the children into their pajamas, and they were busying themselves with wooden blocks. Aunt Mary was napping, as usual. Will was in his office, filling in the ledger for the day. The store had been closed for a couple of hours, and everything was nice and quiet.

Callie opened the book she had retrieved from her suitcase (which she still hadn't unpacked) before she sat down. She had brought it with her to read on the train, but had been too interested in watching all the scenery pass by to bury her nose in a book. Now seemed like the perfect time.

The leather binding made a small creak as she opened it, and the smell of fresh ink and paper wafted to her nostrils. The fire was warm and the chair was comfortable. She flipped to the first page and began to read.

Her reverie was broken by a tugging at her skirt. Callie lifted her book to see Rachel climbing her way into her lap. The tot made herself right at home, snuggling in against Callie. She reached a finger out toward the book still in Callie's hands. "Ooooh," she gurgled as she ran her tiny finger down the page.

It didn't take long for Alexander to abandon the blocks as well. He settled himself at Callie's feet and looked up at her with his big, blue eyes. "Will you read it to us, ma'am?"

Callie smiled in surprise. She had fully planned on having this time to herself, but she couldn't resist this request. "Alright. I had only just started it, so I'll go back to the beginning for you. It's called *Twenty Thousand Leagues Under the Sea,* by Jules Verne."

She read of the adventures of Captain Nemo and the *Nautilus,* pausing every time Alexander had a question and answering him as best she could. Callie was sure that Rachel couldn't understand most of what she read, but the babe seemed to enjoy the sound of her voice. She fell asleep with her cheek pressed into the front of Callie's dress.

"I think your sister is ready for bed," Callie said. "And it's time for you to head there, as well."

Alexander started to protest, but then thought better of it. "Can we read more tomorrow night?" he asked.

Callie nodded. "I'm sure we can arrange that."

As she came back into the living room from tucking the children into their beds, Will was waiting for her by the fireplace. He leaned against the mantle, a distant look in his eyes. The flames lit his face at an angle, making his soft features seem more chiseled. Callie worried that he was upset with her, but then he smiled.

"The young'uns are really taking to you," he said.

She brushed off the compliment. "Oh, well, they were just interested in the book, that's all. I can't blame them; it's a good one."

Will shook his head, his gaze sliding to the Christmas tree. "I think it's more than that. Don't get me wrong; I know my children aren't shy. They can't be with, their papa running a general store. They see all sorts of folks come in and out when they've been behind the counter with me. But it's different with you. Very different."

Callie wasn't sure what to say. She was saved from having to say anything when Will continued on.

"It'll be nice to have a family at Christmastime again." He slipped past her and went to bed, leaving Callie to ponder over what she had done.

Callie had wanted to be a writer for as long as she could remember. She had dreamed of writing fantastic stories about action, adventure, and romance. Heading west seemed to her like the only way to find the peace and inspiration to finally do it. Now that she was here, her fingers itched to write, but not for the same reasons.

She should have gone to sleep herself, but she couldn't stop thinking about how much the children had enjoyed having her reading to them. It was a wonderful feeling to get to share something so special to her with them. The book was a good one, no doubt, but it might have been just a little above Alexander's head. It was most definitely above Rachel's.

With all the rest of the household in bed, Callie felt the itch to write, but not the great epic novel she had envisioned completing once she was ensconced on the prairie. She pulled out several sheets of paper, a pen, and a jar of ink and got to work.

The children needed a story full of life and magic. They needed something that would bring the spirit of Christmas into their hearts. They needed just the right tale, and Callie had it for them. It had to be a good one, after all, because it would be her good-bye gift for them. As set as she had been on some time alone, spending the day with the children had left a warm feeling of satisfaction in her heart. Still, she could not stay here in this house and follow her dream of being a real writer. She tried to shake off the pang of guilt she felt for leaving the children.

And for leaving Will ... When he had simply been an advertisement for a mail order bride, she had no qualms about using his money to make her way out west before she canceled the contract. Actually meeting him, however, with his friendly and undemanding demeanor and his great need for a helpmate, made things much more difficult.

As she wrote on, she wondered what Will would think of her writing. Her family back home had never approved. They felt that her time could be spent doing much more productive things, like finding a husband. She hoped Will wouldn't feel the same way.

No. It doesn't matter what he thinks, because I'm not staying.

She worked into the wee hours of the morning, crafting and weaving her story until it was just right. Just as she nearly had it finished, she ran out of paper. Not ready to give up, Callie looked around. *There must be something around here that will do.*

She knew she could probably slip into the shop and find a packet of stationary, but then she spied the open door to Will's office.

She tiptoed in, not wanting to wake the rest of the household with her movements. The top of Will's desk was immaculate, with not a thing on it other than a stoppered bottle of ink. For a lack of options, Callie slid one of the drawers open. A small sheaf of paper lay inside, and she picked it up. Underneath was Will's ledger book. Callie knew she shouldn't look. She had already come in here without asking, and it would be terribly rude of her to peek at the finances of someone else's business. *A business that I want nothing to do with,* she reminded herself sharply. But her fingers didn't seem to listen as they lifted the ledger from the drawer and casually flipped it open.

Will had every detail of the store lined out in his neat handwriting. Though Callie had never had anything to do with the accounting for her brother-in-law's store, she could easily interpret this book. She skimmed down the page of sales and orders, the price of each written in the second column and the overall profit on the far right. The last two pages of these were all negative.

Callie felt a metallic taste fill her mouth. Even with her incomplete knowledge, she knew those minus signs were a bad, bad thing. She hastily snapped the ledger book closed and carefully replaced it in the drawer, putting most of the sheets of paper back over it except the one she needed to finish her story. She skittered out of Will's office, trying to forget what she had seen.

Aunt Mary's moment of lucid wakefulness the next morning could not have come at a better time. Will had disappeared into the shop shortly after breakfast, and the children were playing happily on the floor. Aunt Mary watched them with her cloudy blue eyes, a smile set firmly in her wrinkled face.

"You seem to be doing well this morning," Callie told her.

The old woman's smile deepened. "I have my good days and my bad," she wheezed. "Mostly bad, but it makes me enjoy the good ones even more."

"I'm glad to hear that."

"So do you love my Will?" Aunt Mary asked.

The question was so sudden that Callie thought at first she didn't hear her right. She searched for the right answer. She couldn't reveal her original plan, especially since she hadn't been able to follow through with it thus far. But she hated the idea of leading this family on further.

"Because I think he's falling in love with you," Mary interjected into Callie's thoughts. "I've seen the look on his face when he watches you and you aren't looking."

She laughed, a breathless, wheezing sort of noise. "I may seem to be out of it most of the time, but I know a spark when I see one."

Callie quickly changed the subject back to Mary's health. "Since you do seem to be having a good day, do you think you could watch the children for just a little bit this morning? I'd like to step out and, ah, get some air."

Aunt Mary nodded her grey head. "Sure, sure. Nothing would make me happier."

Callie didn't give her a chance to change her mind or question her further before she had her purse and was through the door to the shop. Will accepted her excuse just as easily as Aunt Mary did.

"I'm sorry that I can't go with you," he said. "And I'm sorry I've kept you cooped up here for the last couple of days. I suppose I haven't played the part of a host very well, since I didn't even give you a tour of the town." He shook his head at himself.

"It's fine, really," Callie protested. "I don't mind exploring on my own. I won't be long." She swept through the front door and out onto the street.

Cheyenne was a busy town, even in December. Carts and wagons sped through the main road, full of folks gathering supplies before they headed out into the wilderness of Wyoming. There were more stores, shops, and offices than Callie would have dreamed possible in a town like this, which had sprung up fairly recently once the railroad had made its way through. She noticed that they weren't the only general store in town, and that there were in fact at least two others that were fairly close. Customers filed in and out of them at a steady pace. The store windows were decorated with pine boughs and signs calling to customers to buy store bought Christmas gifts. The people who came out had their arms laden down with packages tied up in brown paper and string. Callie paused on the side of the street to watch, and thought about what little she had seen of the running of Will's store so far. He had customers, but the bell over the door wasn't ringing nearly as often as it was for these other stores. This certainly couldn't have been helping out his ledger, but she felt like there was something more to the story.

Moving on, Callie found the storefront she needed. The smell of Smithton's Print Shop was strong, the scent of the ink and the various chemicals they used burning Callie's nose. The big man that stepped out from behind the printing press seemed too large to even fit into the small space, but he had an equally large smile that made Callie feel as though she had come to the right place. He accepted the coins from her savings with pleasure, and promised her the job would be done by Christmas Eve.

Callie wove her way through the crowds and back to the store. She smiled to herself despite the cold, excited about the project she had started. But as she came through the door to find that there was nobody inside save Will, her smile faded. It was time to talk to him.

"Will?"

"Hmmm?" He didn't turn around from rearranging a stack of crates in the corner. "Did you have a nice walk?"

"What? Oh, yes. Yes, I did." Her stomach tumbled inside her. "And I'd like to talk to you. I have some ideas about the store."

This time he did turn around, and he eyed her curiously. "Oh? I'm sorry, I didn't realize that you were interested in the store. Granted, there's a lot of work to do in the house, what with the children and all, and I did imagine you would be helping me out on that end the most, but if you're wanting to work the counter a day or two, perhaps—"

"No," she interrupted his rambling. "I really don't want to work the counter at all. It's just that I have some ideas for getting more customers in here. I saw how busy the other stores in town are, and there's no reason this one shouldn't be the same way. We could decorate the front windows, and I'd be happy to make some signs. You could do a special Christmas sale, perhaps, that would help draw people in."

Will glared at her, a look she hadn't seen yet. "Callie, just what on Earth do you know about running a general store? I had this place going for quite some time before you came along."

Callie felt her cheeks burning in rage and embarrassment. He had no right to dismiss her suggestions so quickly. "I know quite a bit about it, thank you very much. I helped my brother-in-law with his store back in Philadelphia, doing just the sorts of things I mentioned. He had a booming business, so much so that they didn't want me to leave."

His face softened, but just by a little bit. "Why didn't you tell me that?"

Callie felt bold. "Why didn't you tell me your store is in trouble?"

Will paled. "How do you know about that?"

"I saw your ledger. I didn't really mean to, but I was looking for paper when I came across it. I know, I shouldn't have looked. But I did, and I can't change that." She paused a moment, caught between reason and emotions. "I'm sorry."

He sighed and stepped forward to take her hand. "I'm sorry, too. Callie, perhaps I should have told you about the store. I've invested a lot in this place, but I was confident it would pay off. Cheyenne is a busy place, and I never imagined I would have any trouble making that money back. But things don't always go the way you expect, and the store hasn't done all that well with competitors just down the street. When my wife got sick and I called in every doctor around to try and save her, it drained what little I had left. I've been struggling along ever since, hoping for a good month to turn it all around before I have to close the place."

Callie nodded, searching his blue eyes and finding nothing but honesty. "And I suppose that's why there were no Christmas decorations?"

"I scraped up what little I had to get them each a gift. I figured that would mean more to them than the tree." He looked down at their joined hands, and ran his thumb along the back of hers. "I never would have dreamed of doing what you did. You're an amazing woman, Callie. Perhaps I had no right to ask for a wife, but I needed you. My children needed a mother."

"You could have just told me," she said gently. "I know you don't know me, Will, but the money doesn't matter to me that much. And I can help you. I won't tell you that I have any interest in the day-to-day running of the store. I've been forced into that position before and I don't intend to do it again. But I would be more than happy to help you save your store."

"And you aren't upset that I can't afford to get you a wedding dress right now?"

"Not at all." As she stood there in the empty store staring into this sweet man's face, she felt conflicted. She wanted to tell him that she didn't need a wedding dress. He'd opened up to her, and he deserved the truth from her as well. Instead, she turned away from him and got to work on the windows.

Callie pressed her ear to the shop door, waiting. She had spent a decent part of the previous day decorating the front windows of the store. She'd carefully arranged pine boughs around the trim, weaving more strands of popcorn and berries into them as she went. She planned out several ideas for holiday signs, and ran each of them by Will before she made them. He had agreed that taking a slight cut on the profits would be worth it if it would entice more customers to come in the door, and so the price on the most common holiday items had been cut. Callie's signs proudly announced their sale items, including sugar, candy, nuts, fine cloth, and toys. She arranged the items themselves in the windows as well to show potential customers just what they would be getting.

She had barely slept the night before, wondering if her schemes could work. Could she really save his store? Was it possible, or had they waited until it was too close to Christmas, when most of the shopping had already been done?

Now she waited for the bell over the door to start ringing. She knew she would probably be able to hear it just fine as she went about her household duties, but she was too eager. She pressed her ear harder to the wood, hoping and waiting. Concentrating on the shop, she didn't hear what Alexander said behind her until he repeated himself.

"The porridge is burning."

Callie whirled away from the door and back to the stove, using her apron to pull the pan of scorched porridge off the stove. Smoke curled up from the pan, and Callie waved it away with her hand as she coughed. She dropped it onto the table with a clatter, peering inside as she stirred it with the wooden spoon.

"I think it will be alright. Only the bottom burned, so I'll just serve you off the top, shall I?"

The children dug in as though nothing had happened, and Callie resumed her waiting. She pricked her ears as she scrubbed the porridge pan and listened intently as she brought in firewood. By the time she had swept the floors, she had yet to hear the bell.

Dejected, she decided it was time to go apologize to Will. He had put his faith in her, more faith than she felt she deserved, and she had let him down. Just as she placed her hand on the door to the shop, the bell sounded. It was a beautiful sound, light and happy as it rang in a customer. Callie yanked her hand off the door, not wanting to disturb whoever it was that had come to do their shopping.

By noon, the bell had rung more times than Callie could keep track of. She had stopped herself several times from peeking into the store to see how Will was doing. She imagined a store full of customers, bundled up in their winter clothes against the December chill, emptying the barrel of nuts by the scoopful and asking for dolls and blocks to be wrapped up for their young ones. She didn't, however, want to disturb him at his work, until Aunt Mary gave her the perfect excuse.

"I'll bet that boy's getting hungry," she said from her seat by the fire.

Callie thought at first that Mary was talking of Alexander, who had just finished a hearty meal of ham, bread, and beans. She moved on with her work, assuming it was another of Aunt Mary's rants.

"I kept telling him to hire help, but he won't do it," Mary continued. "I don't know why. Stubborn thing. I guess he'll just starve himself until closing time."

Realizing the truth of Aunt Mary's words, Callie quickly made a sandwich out of the remaining ham and slipped into the store. Will was behind the counter with his back to her. Callie's imagination had not been far off. A young woman was happily watching her two young daughters admire the dolls. An elderly gentleman was busily filling a bag with nuts. Will was ringing up another gentleman at the counter.

Not wanting to distract him, Callie placed the sandwich on the counter where Will would be sure to see it when he finished with his customer. She turned to go, but a hand grabbed her by the elbow. She turned back to see Will's blue eyes staring into hers.

"Thank you," he said with a smile.

Callie nodded and stepped back into the house.

Christmas Eve settled on the Stanton household with a feeling of warmth and excitement. The other general stores in town had closed for the holiday, but Will had kept his open. The children protested at first, but he quickly explained his reasoning.

"I don't have to stand at the counter all day. I can be right here at home with you children, and I'll just step into the store if the bell rings. I doubt anyone will come, anyway. They won't expect me to be open."

But he spent far less time with his family than anyone ever would have expected. The shop was bustling with folks who hadn't bought quite as much flour as they actually needed or were snapping up a quick extra gift for someone special. By the time Will fell back into the house at the end of the day, he looked exhausted and satisfied.

"This has just been incredible," he said as he sat down at the table for his dinner. "I think I did more business in two days than I did in the last two months! I even had a man come in today that didn't need anything. He said he came in simply because he saw that I was open, and he bought several bolts of cloth for his wife." Will shook his head in wonder as he tucked into his food. "I think I might actually have to hire some help if this keeps up.

Aunt Mary nodded and smiled.

When the table had been cleared and the children were ready for bed, Callie called them over to her. She pulled a slim book off the mantle and sat in one of the chairs by the fire.

"I know you are excited to see what presents you'll get in the morning, but your present from me comes tonight."

She opened the book and began to read. The child sat in rapt attention as they listened to the tale of Christmas fairies, magic, and sparkling snow. Rachel laid her head on Callie's shoulder as she listened, her eyelids drooping a little with each turn of the page. When she was done, Callie asked them what they thought of the story.

Rachel nodded her head sleepily, but Alexander had a hard time holding back his enthusiasm. "It was wonderful!" he exclaimed. "But I have a question."

"Of course."

"Why is your name on the cover?"

Callie turned the book over to look at the front cover. The title, *The Magic of Christmas,* was imprinted into the leather, with "Callie Browning" just below it. She felt a thrill of energy spark up her back. It wasn't the great American novel she had envisioned, but it really meant something to her. Especially since it meant something to these children.

"Well, I wrote it," she explained to Alexander. "When the printer makes the book, he always puts the author's name on the cover so you know who wrote it."

"Wow," Alexander breathed as he took the book from Callie's hands to examine it more closely. "Have you written other books? Did you write *Twenty Thousand Leagues Under the Sea?*"

Callie laughed. "No, I sure didn't. Mabye I'll write more books someday, but for right now this is the only one I have. And actually, it's for the two of you to keep. Merry Christmas."

"Alright, you two," Will intervened. "It's about time to get on up to bed if you want Santa Clause to come leave you presents."

It took no more than that to make the children forget about their new book and scamper into their beds. Callie tucked them each in with a kiss and a hug before she returned to the living room, where Will was waiting for her.

"I had no idea you could write like that, Callie," he said. "You've surprised me at every turn. First, you made beautiful decorations with my children. Then, you brought my store back to life. That alone I never would have thought possible. But to see that you have such talent in you, that you can write like that …"

"I didn't know you were listening."

"I couldn't help myself! It was a remarkable story. Tell me; did you just have the one copy printed, or are there more?"

"Oh, there's just the one. It was just a little thing I did for the children. It's not a big deal. Just a silly dream I always had about becoming a writer." Heat rose in her cheeks, but not from the fireplace.

Will came across the room and took each of her hands in his. "It most certainly is a big deal. And I think it's safe to say that you already are a writer. We can have more of those printed up for next Christmas, and you can make a display of them in the front window. Most people do go to the printer's for their books, but I'm sure we'll sell plenty of copies when folks are here for their other items. The books will help bring people in the store for the holidays, like you did this year."

Callie studied his face. He had been nothing but kind since she had arrived in Cheyenne, and she could still see that. But now there was something more, something that made him seem more alive. Her heart leapt toward him, bouncing against the confines of her ribcage.

"My goodness, Callie," he breathed. "What other secrets do you hold?"

"Oh, Will." He had no idea just what he was asking of her. The truth was going to hurt him, but it was time to tell it. "I'm afraid I do have another secret. This one, though, is not one that will make you happy, or proud, or successful." She buried her face in her hands. "I'm so ashamed."

He wrapped his arms tighter around her. "It's alright, Callie. You can tell me anything. I promise it won't change the way I feel about you."

She sighed into his chest. "You mentioned that you hadn't been completely honest in your advertisement, and I can't say that I was, either. I told you that I had never been married and had no children, and that much was true. But I didn't really want to come out West to find a husband. I wanted to get away from my life in Philadelphia. I wanted to start over, to live for myself instead of for someone else all the time. I wanted to write." Tears began to trickle down her cheeks.

"It's alright, Callie. I understand. Everyone needs a fresh start sometimes."

"But I was so selfish, Will. I was going to come to Cheyenne, and then ask you to nullify the contract. I was never going to marry you."

"Oh. I see." He dropped his arms to his sides and took a step back. "Well, then. I suppose that explains why you weren't bothered about not having a wedding dress. I won't be able to take you to the train station tomorrow. They'll be closed for Christmas. But I promise I'll take you the day after."

"No, Will. I—"

"It's alright, Callie. We each had our own motivations. I'm not going to make you feel like you have to stay here. I don't want you to live the rest of your life and not see your dreams realized."

"That's the thing, Will. You've made me understand that I still can live my dreams, and I don't have to sacrifice everything else in order to do it. I thought I would never be able to write if I had all the responsibilities of a household on my shoulders. And I definitely thought that helping run a general store would be in my way. Coming here and spending a few days with you and your children, and even Aunt Mary, has shown me that I don't need to run away from it all. I just need to be around the right people, people that inspire me. And that's you, Alexander, and Rachel."

"What are you saying, Callie?" Will's eyebrows knit together in concern and, Callie thought, hope.

"I don't want to leave. I don't want to run away anymore. I want to stay, here, with you. If you'll have me, that is."

He stepped back toward her and put his arms around her once again. "I would like nothing more."

She leaned into his warm embrace for a moment, then looked up at his smiling face. "Well, I guess I better start shopping for a wedding dress."

"Yes, I guess we better," Will grinned. "Merry Christmas, Callie."

"Merry Christmas, Will," she replied, thinking of the great stories they were going to write together.

OTHER BOOKS IN THIS SERIES

If you loved this story why not continue straight away with other books in the series?

A Surprise Christmas Bride For The Heartbroken Widower

A Headstrong Christmas Bride for the Lonely Father

A Desperate Christmas Bride for the Cold Hearted Rancher

A Spoiled Christmas Bride for the Struggling Cowboy

A Clever Christmas Bride for the Burdened Shop Owner

A Curious Christmas Bride for the Cautious Sheriff

A Pregnant Christmas Bride for the Bad Mannered Brick Layer

A Reluctant Christmas Family for the Gentle Horseman

An Unexpected Christmas Baby for the Brokenhearted Blacksmith

A Sudden Christmas Family for the Hesitant Rancher

A Lonely Christmas Bride for the Solitary Miner

A Pair of Christmas Sisters for the Lumberjack Brothers

OR READ THE COMPLETE BOXSET!

Available On Amazon

Read Now

OUR GIFT TO YOU

AS A WAY TO SAY THANK YOU WE WOULD LOVE TO SEND YOU THIS BEAUTIFUL TRILOGY FREE OF CHARGE.

Our Reader List is 100% FREE

Click here to claim your free Historical Western trilogy... **https://pureread.com/western**

At PureRead we publish books you can trust. Great tales without smut or swearing, but with all of the mystery and romance you expect from a great story.

Be the first to know when we release new books, take part in our fun competitions, and get surprise free books in your inbox by signing up to our Reader list.

As a thank you you'll receive this exclusive Western trilogy - a beautiful collection available only to our subscribers...

Click here to claim your free Historical Western trilogy... **https://**

Made in the USA
Middletown, DE
21 February 2023